GHOST TWINS

THE MYSTERY ON WALRUS MOUNTAIN

Dian Curtis Regan

AN
APPLE
PAPERBACK

D1491060

SCHOLASTIC INC.
New York Toronto London Auckland Sydney

ISBN 0-590-48255-6

Copyright © 1995 by Dian Curtis Regan.
Map illustration copyright © 1994 by Cindy Knox.
All rights reserved. Published by Scholastic Inc.
APPLE PAPERBACKS is a registered trademark of Scholastic Inc.

12 11 10 9 8 7 6 5 4 3 2 1   5 6 7 8 9/9 0/0

Printed in the U.S.A.   40

First Scholastic printing, January 1995

With fond memories of Avery Morrell French

Contents

1.	The Mysterious Box	1
2.	Funny Names	8
3.	Funny Games	13
4.	Good-bye Blue Skier	20
5.	Into the Great White Open	26
6.	Breaking the Barrier	30
7.	Crashing and Burning	37
8.	Disaster at Blaze's Burgers	44
9.	Look Who's Talking	52
10.	Robbie versus Killer Mountain	58
11.	Wild Ride	66
12.	The Snow Monster	72
13.	U O Me 1	77
14.	Beka's Midnight Message	84
15.	Don't Look Down	90
16.	The Race	97
17.	Number 31, Who Are You?	100
18.	The Pink Vulture	103
19.	Not Again!	106
20.	Going for the Gold	109
21.	The Final Message	113

Friday, August 25, 1944   *5 cents*

JUNIPER DAILY NEWS

New Fall Fashions Inside!

Twins Involved in Boating Mishap

Robert Adam Zuffel and his twin sister, Rebeka Allison, seem to be victims of a boating accident at Kickingbird Lake. Their dog, Thatch, disappeared with them. Family members say that the twins had gone hiking on Mystery Island and were probably returning when yesterday's windstorm blew in.

Their overturned canoe was floating in the water off Mystery Island. A party of family members searched the lake and the surrounding area, but no trace of the twins or their dog was found.

Today's Highlights

President Roosevelt Welcomes Cary Grant to White House . . pg.2

Zoot Suits All the Rage pg.3

Movie Review: *Bambi* pg.5

Local Student Wins Award for Model of All 48 States pg.6

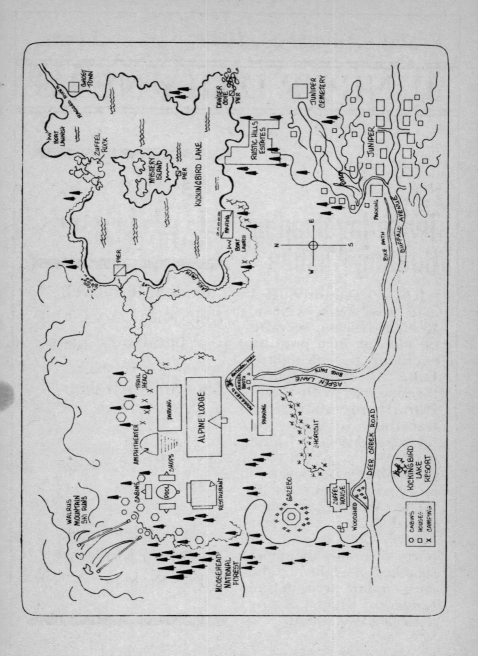

1

The Mysterious Box

"What is it?" Beka whispered. Her words were sprinkled with awe.

Robbie leaned around the Zuffel house's newest guest to study the strange contraption the boy was eagerly plugging in. "I don't know."

Whatever it was, it made Robbie curious.

The boy seemed to be the same age as the twins. But he was smaller — and quicker, untangling wires and adjusting equipment with a speed that amazed Robbie.

His hair was long. One curl hung in his eyes. Robbie wondered if his brisk movements kept him from sitting still long enough for a barber to cut it.

"Looks like the box with the moving pictures

in the family room," Beka said, moving out of the boy's way. "The one they call TV."

"A TV sitting on top of a typewriter, you mean."

Thatch, whose curiosity was worse than a cat's, hopped onto the desk chair and did some serious sniffing of the mysterious box.

Beka nudged Thatch out of the way. "You let a stranger move into Robbie's old bedroom without so much as a growl?" she teased. "Is this your day off as watchdog?"

With a quick jerk, the boy straightened. Shoving hair from his eyes, his gaze darted about the room. Had he sensed the presence of the ghost twins? And their dog?

How could he not? They were practically standing in the same spot, trying to get a good look at whatever he was assembling.

With a visible shiver, the boy moved to the bed. Digging through a messy suitcase, he lifted out a heavy sweater and pulled it on.

"Sorry you find our presence so chilling," Beka sniffed. "You're not such a warm guy yourself. Haven't even told us your name."

Robbie stopped inspecting the small TV screen to chuckle at his sister.

"Noah!" came a voice from downstairs.

"His name is Noah," Robbie told her.

"I heard."

"Yeah, Dad?"

"Five minutes!"

Noah shoved the suitcase out of the way and dumped some square plastic disks onto the bed. "I'm not going!" he hollered back. "I'm staying here to do my homework. I have to write an article."

Sounds of heavy boots clumped up the stairs and around the second-floor landing.

"Oh, great," Noah mumbled. In one swift move, he was back at the desk with one of the disks. After he clicked a switch, the box made a *dinging* sound while the screen flashed a rainbow of colors. He shoved the disk into a slot, then began talking to the screen and punching keys.

Noah's father stepped into the room. His face was tan. Sunglasses perched on top of his head. The rest of him was lost in a bulky jacket.

"You'll have plenty of time to set up your travel computer and do your homework," he said. "Right now, we're heading up to Moosehead. The carnival's already started. It'll be fun."

"Computer," Robbie echoed. "He called it a computer."

Noah made a face when his father wasn't looking. "But I'd rather — "

"Noah Grindelwald French."

"*Grindelwald?*" Beka wrinkled her nose. "What kind of a middle name is *that?*"

"Hey!" came another voice from downstairs.

"Coming!" Mr. French called. "Get your coat and boots on." With that he hurried from the room.

"Rats." Noah clicked off the screen. The computer spit out the disk. Snatching it, he tossed it onto the bed.

Thatch dove.

"Hey, don't toss things around my dog." Robbie intercepted Thatch before he could get his teeth around the disk. "He could crunch this in two like a cookie."

Noah lifted a jacket off the back of a chair. "If I go up to the carnival," he said in a grumbly voice, "first person I'll run into is Zip Boston."

"Zip Boston? These people have *strange* names." Beka distracted Thatch so he'd leave Noah's things alone. "Think we should let them stay in our house?"

"Only if they offer an explanation," Robbie said, tailing Noah out the door.

"About their names?" Beka asked, following.

"And about the strange machine in my bedroom. The computer."

"It's not your bedroom anymore," she reminded him. "The attic is."

"I know." Robbie would *never* get used to other kids in his old bedroom.

Downstairs, Noah's mother held the front door open, acting impatient. "We're wasting a beautiful day. Let's join the festivities and unpack later."

The twins and Thatch hustled out the door with the others.

Bright sunlight reflected off a fresh layer of snow, making Robbie squint. The front yard of the Zuffel house, framed by a row of trees bordering Deer Creek Road, looked like a postcard photo.

"Are we taking the car?" Noah asked.

"No, let's walk." His mom started off along the drive that curved out to the road. "Walking through drifts will help build your leg muscles." Her snow-white smile sparkled against a face as tan as her husband's.

Pulling the hood of her jacket over her hair, she led the pack past Mr. Tavolott's workers as they shoveled the drive. Mr. Tavolott was the owner of Kickingbird Lake Resort.

Noah began to limp as he walked. He pressed a hand against his right thigh, as though it bothered him.

"Was he limping in his room?" Robbie remembered how quick Noah's movements had been.

Beka raised an eyebrow in suspicion. "No, he *wasn't* limping."

Robbie glanced at his sister, slogging through snow in her shirtsleeves, plaid skirt, and saddle shoes — the same clothes she'd worn for fifty years. Yet, even if they were here *another* fifty, he'd never get over the wonder of not feeling cold, or hunger, or pain — now that they were ghosts.

Robbie watched Thatch gallop ahead. He didn't know he was a ghost dog, but it didn't stop him from loving the snow. He leaped over drifts — or burrowed through them — until the fur on his face sparkled with ice crystals.

Mr. French looped an arm across his son's shoulders. "Change your mind yet about the junior ski race?"

"Nope."

The answer came quickly, Robbie noticed.

"But Dr. Faruka said you were ready to start training, and — "

"I said *no*." Noah's stubbornness came through loud and clear.

"Well, we brought your skis just in case you change your mind."

Mrs. French's arm went around his shoulders, too. "You know, this is where your father won his

6

first ski race when he was your age. A gold medallion with a blue satin rib — "

Robbie caught up with them. Why had she stopped speaking so abruptly?

Noah fell back from the group at the same time Mr. French sped up.

"Sorry," his mom said in a quiet voice. "I forgot."

"Forgot what?" Robbie was intrigued. "Tell me about the gold medallion."

"Yeah," Beka added, catching up with him. "I want to hear, too."

But Noah and his parents were quiet as they turned up Aspen Lane.

"Hmmmm." Robbie threw an "invisible" snowball at Thatch. "I think we have a mystery on our hands."

"*Woof!*" An excited Thatch forgot the snowball and trotted back to Robbie. *Mystery* was a people word the ghost dog understood.

2
Funny Names

Aspen Lane was bursting with Kickingbird Lake shuttle vans, cars, trucks, jeeps, and people on the footpath — all heavily bundled against the cold.

As the group neared the archway to Moosehead National Park, Robbie saw two park rangers balancing on ladders, stringing a banner across the arch. It read:

WELCOME TO WALRUS MOUNTAIN
WINTER CARNIVAL!

The famous mountain, from a distance, resembled a walrus because two ski runs cut through the pines like long tusks.

Robbie grabbed Thatch's collar so he wouldn't lose track of him as they wandered past the lodge, then among shops and cafés. Light posts and railings sported bright decorations: balloons, colored lights, and plastic streamers.

Red-nosed clowns and mimes (with faces as ghost-white as the twins') moved through the crowd, giving away trinkets and treats and making people laugh.

West of Alpine Lodge, a skating rink buzzed with excited voices. Experienced skaters in tights and twirly skirts zipped past unexperienced skaters in bulky clothes, creeping along the edges of the rink.

A junior park ranger handed Mr. French a program listing the weekend activities. He passed it to Noah. "Look, Son, skating competitions, cross-country ski races, snowboarding, tobogganing — this should keep you entertained while your mother and I practice for our race."

Noah shrugged, shoving the schedule into his pocket.

"Let's get some hot cocoa," his mom suggested. She pointed toward an outdoor stand selling drinks and snacks.

"Sounds great," Robbie told her. "We want cocoa, too, with lots of tiny marshmallows."

Beka poked him in the ribs.

Mrs. French handed money to Noah. "Go get three cups while we find a table."

Noah headed toward the stand. Moments later, a girl at the head of the line paid for her hot dog, then moved through the crowd, bumping into Noah. The blow knocked him off his feet.

Robbie thought she'd done it on purpose.

Noah sprawled on the crusty layer of snow, scowling up at the girl. "I was afraid I'd see you here."

Robbie started to help Noah up, then realized he couldn't. Sometimes he forgot he was a ghost.

"Of course I'm here," the girl said. "I'm here to win first place in the junior ski race." She waved the hot dog around as she talked.

Thatch noticed the waving frankfurter. After all, hot dog was his middle name.

Noah came to his feet, shaking the leg that seemed to bother him. "You wouldn't win," he told her, "if *I* was skiing this year."

"Right." She looked him up and down. "So why *aren't* you skiing this year? I don't see the crutches anymore."

Noah squirmed in place, obviously uncomfortable with her question. "I'm, um, still recovering." He hurried on before she could respond. "Just wait. I'll beat you fair and square some day."

"I don't think so," the girl said.

Then she made a mistake.

She let the arm holding the hot dog dangle at her side.

At her side hunched Thatch. Waiting. All he had to do was stretch his shaggy neck and snatch the hot dog out of the bun.

Which was exactly what he did.

"Thatch!" Robbie yelled, but he couldn't keep from laughing. The girl deserved it for being mean to Noah.

"You'll never beat me, Grindelwald."

Noah cringed.

So did Robbie.

"They don't call me Zip for nothing."

The girl breezed past him, looking smug. Then she chomped down on an empty hot dog bun. The smug look traded places with surprise and confusion.

Score one for Thatch.

"Zip?" Beka said. *"That* was Zip Boston?"

Robbie was still sympathizing with Noah. He knew how it felt when a girl found out your middle name. In the fourth grade, Lucy Moreno had found out *his* middle name.

Adam. *Adam* wasn't nearly as weird as *Grindelwald*. Still, Lucy had teased him and Beka, calling them *Adam* and *Eve* until Robbie wanted to buy her a one-way ticket on a hot-air blimp.

The twins followed Noah back to the table.

"Why don't you think he wants to compete in the junior ski race?" Beka leaned against a decorated light pole. "Sounds like he used to compete."

"Must have something to do with his leg." Robbie watched with envy while the Frenches sipped their steaming cocoa. "I'll bet Noah was injured."

"Well, *I* think he's faking," Beka sniffed. "He moved pretty fast in his room when nobody was watching. I think it's all in his *head*, not his leg."

"Or," Robbie added, "*maybe* it has something to do with a terror of a rival named Zip Boston."

3
Funny Games

"**H**er real name is Susie."

Robbie glanced up from the lower bunk bed where he was relaxing with a ghost dog sprawled across his stomach. The attic bedroom was their special place — now that the old Zuffel house was a vacation rental with lots of people coming and going on the lower floors.

"*Whose* name?"

"Zip Boston's." Beka was sitting on the braided rug between the bunk beds and the dresser, reading a *Walrus Mountain Winter Carnival* brochure she'd snitched from the ranger station.

She'd also snitched trinkets from a clown, which, she reasoned, was okay since he was giving them away. Her wrists and hands were adorned with three bracelets and two rings.

It took a lot of concentration for the ghosts to move things from the "real" world into their dimension. But once they did, the objects became invisible to people.

"Listen to this," Beka said. "Under *Entrants for the Junior Ski Race*, it says: 'Number 15, Susie Boston, ranked in the top ten.' "

"Wow!" Robbie was impressed. "Is Noah's name there?"

Beka peered at the list. "Yep. He's in the top ten, too, but there's an X next to his name, which means he's not competing this year."

"Because of his injury?"

"Doesn't say." She studied the page. "I wonder what happened?"

Robbie didn't have an answer.

Beka tossed the brochure to him. "So, what do *you* want to compete in? Snowboarding? Ice-skating? The toboggan run?"

"Ha," Robbie said. The winter sport *I'm* best at is sliding down the mountain on my bottom — then drinking gallons of hot cocoa."

"Not an event," Beka laughed.

Robbie shoved Thatch off his stomach. "Let's go downstairs and see if Noah's working on that TV thing yet."

"Computer," Beka said, correcting him.

The trio hurried to Noah's bedroom. The room wasn't as messy as it'd been this morning. His clothes and suitcase were neatly stowed. Now he hunched at the desk, clicking away on the typewriter that sat in front of the screen.

Thatch immediately claimed the bed, falling onto his side, making lots of sleepy doggie noises.

Noah's mom followed the twins into the room. (Of course, she didn't *know* she'd followed the twins into the room.)

She'd changed into a matching jacket and bulky pants with zippers up the sides of the legs. The material was slick, shiny yellow. It reminded Robbie of the dustcovers his grandmother used to throw over furniture in her summer cottage whenever she went away.

"Are you working on your article for school?" Mrs. French asked.

The instant he heard his mother's voice, Noah's fingers danced over the keys. "Open Homework file," he said.

The computer obeyed.

"Raz, did you see that?" Beka used the nickname formed from their shared initials. "The computer does what he tells it to."

He nodded, not wanting to miss anything Noah did.

When the computer stopped churning, Noah

15

pointed to the screen, giving proof to his mother he was doing what he was *supposed* to be doing.

Robbie suspected Noah had been working on something else.

Something that looked an awful lot like a game.

Was he playing a game on the TV screen? A game he could control by tapping keys, twirling the stationary ball on the keyboard, and speaking to the screen? "Nifty," Robbie mumbled, wanting to see more.

"What's your article about?" his mom asked.

"Jean-Claude Killy. Champion ski racer."

She seemed pleased. "Didn't he win the World Cup?"

"He won the very *first* World Cup."

Mrs. French smiled at her son's answer, then twirled her gloves, acting coy. "Did you know I once met Jean-Claude Killy?"

Noah swiveled his chair, facing her. "You did?" Awe filled his voice.

"Yes. On the same trip to Switzerland when I met your father. As you know, we met in the quaint little ski town of — "

"Grindelwald," Noah finished. His smile faded.

"And that's why we named you — "

"I know," he answered dully. "Causing me a lifetime of grief."

"Well, that explains the funny name." Robbie said.

Beka snickered. "Good thing they didn't meet in Kalamazoo."

"Or Timbuktu."

The twins' teasing made Thatch scramble off the bed to join them at Noah's desk. "*Woof!*" he barked.

Robbie took a playful swipe at his dog. "That's the *worst* middle name of all."

Mrs. French gave Noah a quick pat on the head. "Someday you'll think it's romantic that your parents named you after the place they met."

His expression said he didn't agree.

She adjusted the ski goggles hanging around her neck. "Well, your father and I are off for a practice run on the mountain." She paused, giving him a hopeful look. "Would you like to go skiing with us?"

Noah pressed his lips together, which, Robbie assumed, meant the question was one she'd asked often, yet his answer never changed.

"Fine," she said. "Just thought I'd ask. To see if you're ready to come back yet."

"No, I'm not."

"But Dr. Faruka — "

His look stopped her.

"Okay, then. Do your homework, and we'll all go out for a nice dinner tonight."

" 'Bye," Noah said. The instant she was gone, his fingers went to work, blanking the screen full of text, and calling up the game once more.

Robbie drew closer to watch. Instant images appeared, each for a few seconds, then faded into the next: tiny chairs chugged up a mountain slope on cables; lines of flag-topped poles angled down the mountain; white snow; blue sky; evergreens.

Cartoonlike people, dressed in the same kind of outfit Mrs. French had been wearing, waved from a line, as if they were posing for a camera.

Suddenly a horrible monster loomed across the screen. He roared and beat his chest, like King Kong, then turned and chased the skiers.

Robbie and Beka were glued to the screen, waiting to see what would happen next. Even Thatch sat, head cocked, ears up, staring hard.

The next picture showed the same group, now unsmiling, sitting in the dark, scary den of the snow monster. All their arms and legs were in casts.

Then the screen flashed:

Welcome to Killer Mountain
Ski at Your Own Risk.

Robbie couldn't *wait* for Noah to start playing the game.

He couldn't wait to see Noah ski for real, too. Up on Walrus Mountain.

But would he ever see Noah ski?

As long as the boy could sit here safely in his room — skiing inside his computer — why would he *want* to face whatever had scared him so badly out there on the slopes?

4
Good-bye Blue Skier

The game began — with a list of questions.
The screen asked Noah what color he wanted to be.

Noah swiveled the ball on the keyboard. The motion directed an arrow to a ski racer dressed in blue. With his thumb, Noah pressed a bar that made a clicking noise.

There were more questions: What number do you want to be?

Noah clicked on number *1*.

"Ha, he wants to be the best," Beka said.

Pick the difficulty of the race.

Noah clicked on Hardest.

At which speed do you wish to play?

Fastest.

"He must be good," Beka whispered, gazing at the screen as if it held her under a magic spell.

"He must," Robbie agreed. "I would have picked *Easy* and *Slow*."

Next, Noah — or rather the skier dressed in blue tights — took a seat on the chairlift.

Noah hit a key, which made that segment of the game speed up, zooming the skier's chair to the top of the hill.

"He's in a hurry to start," Robbie said, pleased.

The skier took his place, aiming downhill, poles ready to shove off.

A man appeared on the right side of the screen. Pointing a gun in the air, he pulled the trigger. Out of the barrel came a flag with the word BANG! at the same time the computer beeped.

The skier was off, *shussing* down the hill, zig-zagging smoothly between poles. Noah controlled each movement by rolling the ball and tapping keys so fast that his fingers seemed to blur.

Suddenly a tree appeared out of nowhere, blocking the skier's path.

No problem for Noah. He quickly steered the figure around the unexpected obstacle. Beyond the next bend, a mother goose and her goslings waddled across the trail.

"Look out!" Beka yelled, getting caught up in the game.

Thatch went wild barking. He hopped into Noah's lap to get closer.

Robbie tried to pull him down, afraid he'd distract Noah, who'd jumped over the goose family and was flying on down the mountain.

Noah didn't know that a ghost dog was taking up his space in the chair. But Robbie had learned, from past experience, when they got this close to a person — something happened.

Whether the person *felt* their presence, or even *suspected* that ghosts were around, Robbie didn't know. He just knew their *ghostliness* had some kind of affect on people.

Noah punched a PAUSE button. The screen froze, leaving the poor skier in midair. Jumping up, Noah knocked his chair over, Thatch and all. Then he hugged himself, as though the temperature in the room had dropped twenty degrees.

Yanking a jacket from the closet, Noah slipped it on. His eyes moved back and forth, as if waiting to see whether more weird things were going to happen.

"Thatch, look what you've done." Robbie was annoyed at the dog for interrupting the game.

Now Thatch balanced on his hind legs, leaning against the desk so he could keep an eye on the suspended skier.

Noah righted the chair and sat down. With one tap to a key, the game resumed. The blue skier flew downhill, taking every obstacle in stride: hidden rocks, cliffs, bears, and a monkey. (A monkey on a ski slope? Ha!)

Next came moguls. Robbie knew what the snow-covered mounds were called because the computer screen flashed MOGUL ALERT right before the blue skier faced an entire hillside of them.

"Oh, no!" Beka cried. The skier had manipulated a curve and come face-to-face with a little old lady pushing a shopping cart full of groceries.

Thatch began to whine.

In one smooth leap, the skier sailed over the cart, leaving the viewer with a glimpse of the lady's confused face.

Beka laughed. "You don't expect to see these things on a ski slope!" As she said it, a bicycle rider, wearing a hat that read *KILLER MOUNTAIN PIZZA DELIVERY*, almost collided with the skier.

A split second later, a gigantic, fur-covered, sharp-clawed hand darkened the entire sky.

"The snow monster!" Noah yelped.

Frantically, he worked the keyboard, but it was too late.

In a heartbeat, hairy fingers curled around the skier.

The game's dinging alarm bells mixed with Thatch's growling.

The next screen showed the ugly creature, with three evil eyes and fangs as long as ski poles, holding the blue skier up for inspection.

With a growl-laugh that seemed to rattle the whole computer, the snow monster popped the skier into his mouth. His eyes grew large as he spit out the skis and poles.

Next flashed the score:

Killer Mountain: 1   Noah: 0

"I should have seen him coming," Noah grumbled, starting the game over.

This time he picked the red skier and the speed Medium-fast.

The red skier shoved off from the top of the mountain. At first, he zigzagged smoothly across the slope with no obstacles blocking his way.

Then, along the bottom of the screen came a young woman, slowly pushing a baby carriage. The baby peeked out, crying and pointing at the skier the mother hadn't noticed.

Robbie and Beka laughed at the silliness of the game.

Before the red skier could angle around the baby carriage, a barking dog streaked across the screen. He grabbed the mother's coat and tried to tug her and the baby out of harm's way.

"What's *that*?" Noah blurted.

The red skier faltered.

"Is he going to hit them?" Robbie felt disappointed. Was the game over already? Had Killer Mountain scored another point against Noah?

Noah stopped tapping keys and gaped at the screen.

Confused, Robbie waited.

"Look!" Beka cried.

Then Robbie realized why Beka was shouting and jumping up and down.

He caught his breath.

The dog desperately trying to save the woman and baby was *not* part of the computer game. The dog was . . .

"Thatch!" Robbie shouted.

5

Into the Great White Open

Robbie twirled, searching the room for Thatch. He was gone.

Hadn't the dog been here only moments ago? Balancing on his hind legs and resting his front paws on the desk to get closer to the screen?

How had he gone from HERE . . . to THERE? And where *was* THERE?

Another dimension? The great white open?

Beka's nose was inches from the screen. "Raz, we've got to *do* something."

"Yeah, but *what*?" Robbie was fascinated by the possibilities. "How do you think Thatch got in there?"

"*Smooshed*?" Beka offered.

Smooshing was something Thatch had taught

26

them. It came in handy whenever they needed to go *inside* or *outside*, and all doors were closed.

The process worked by changing them from ghosts to . . . well, *ghost clouds* that could swirl through a keyhole, a cracked window, a knothole — any tiny opening.

Smooshing took lots of concentration, though, and always left them with a throbbing headache. Yet if Thatch could go into the computer by *smooshing*, then so could they.

"There's no hole in the screen," Robbie argued.

"But there are holes *below* the screen where the sounds come out," Beka offered. "And what about that slot where Noah put the disk?"

Robbie tried to squelch the fear crawling into his mind. He gave his sister a somber look. "I've got to go after Thatch. No telling what kind of trouble he might get into."

Noah must have pushed PAUSE again because the red skier was frozen midturn at the top of the screen, and the woman and baby were stuck in the middle of the slope.

The only one moving was Thatch.

Noah kept jabbing keys and spinning the ball. "What's wrong with this?" he mumbled.

Beka patted Robbie on the back. "Go get him, Sport."

Robbie wondered about the side effects of making himself the size of a . . . a cough drop. What would it feel like? Then Beka's words sunk in. "Aren't you coming with me?" he asked.

She gave him a worried look. "Don't you think I should stay behind? Just in case?"

"In case what?"

"Umm. In case I have to *bring* you back?" She pointed at the keyboard.

"Good point. *Smooshing in* might be easier than *smooshing out*."

Beka peered at the screen. "Hurry Rob. Before that — that snow monster shows up again."

Robbie shuddered at the thought of the monster swallowing the blue skier. "I was hoping you wouldn't mention him."

"*Him*? It could be a *she*-monster."

"Hush, Beka." What he was about to do was bad enough without his sister making it worse.

"Sorry," she said. "Are you getting cold feet?"

"No, but I will as soon as I hit the slopes." Robbie gave a weak laugh at his own joke. At least it took his mind off what he was about to do.

Positioning himself as close to the computer as he could, he focused on the screen, thankful that Noah was distracted enough to leave the keyboard alone. The boy was paging through the computer manual, searching for the source of the "problem."

Focus, Robbie told himself. *Concentrate*. He

waited for dizziness to sweep over him — a signal that the act of *smooshing* was about to begin.

Nothing happened.

"Help me," Robbie hissed.

The twins' powers were greater when they combined their efforts.

Beka had been reading the manual over Noah's shoulder. She turned her attention toward the screen, resting a finger on one of the keys. Robbie didn't know what she was doing, but he didn't allow it to break his focus.

Yes, he told himself. *Concentrate.* Annoyed at distractions, he rubbed the side of his face, which had started to tingle. The tingling spread down his neck and filled his chest. Then he realized it was happening.

A tidal wave of dizziness crashed inside his head. Icicles pricked every inch of his skin. A gust of frigid wind *whooshed* through the room.

Then a monster roared in Robbie's ears. He only hoped it *wasn't* the snow monster.

6
Breaking the Barrier

"*N*ow what?" Noah grumbled, frowning first at the instruction manual, then the screen. "There's *another* figure. A boy. Where did *he* come from?"·

"Wow." Beka was amazed. "He did it. He went into the game. And Noah can *see* him and Thatch. As clearly as I can."

For a moment, she and Noah stayed frozen to the screen, watching Robbie try to convince the dog to leave the game lady and the baby alone.

Robbie kept touching his head. Beka wondered if he was suffering the aftereffect of a *smooshing* headache.

The room was silent. Except for the soft hum

of the computer, and the sound of Thatch's barking.

Thatch's barking!

Suddenly it sank in to Beka's mind.

"I can *hear* Thatch! Which means, I can probably hear Robbie, too." She stopped to listen. Robbie was talking to Thatch all right, but his words were faint mumbles. "The question is — can Noah hear him?"

The thought that Robbie could talk to Noah through the computer was so exciting, Beka felt like hugging this odd machine that could spin magic.

"I give up," Noah said. He tossed the manual onto the desk, and placed his fingers on the keys.

Beka panicked. Was he planning to shut off the machine? What would happen to Robbie and Thatch? Losing them forever on Killer Mountain was *not* an idea she wanted to consider.

"Wait!" she yelped. What could she do to stop him? She *had* to make Robbie talk to Noah. But how?

Could he hear her? Could she talk to the computer the way Noah did, and make Robbie understand?

Noah was hesitating, as if terribly fascinated by the game's apparent "malfunction."

31

"Robbie!" Beka hollered. "Say something. Talk to Noah. I think he can hear you."

Robbie looked up at them. Right *at* them! Holding Thatch by the collar, he waved. "Noah!" he cried. "Can you hear me?"

Noah came out of his chair so fast, it appeared that someone had jerked him out by the collar. "What's going on?" he hissed.

"Rob, explain all this to him."

He got the message. "I'm Robbie Zuffel," he began. "This is my dog Thatch. He got into your game and I came in to bring him back."

"Zuffel," Noah whispered, as if the name sounded familiar.

"Like in Zuffel house," Beka told him. "*This* house."

"Um." Robbie glanced nervously around. The game mother and baby carriage were still frozen in place. So was the red skier. "You *can* bring us back, can't you, Noah?"

Suddenly Noah came to life. "Where'd you come from?"

"Good question," Robbie answered. "I live in the house where you're staying. Only you can't see me there because I'm . . . uh . . . a ghost."

"A ghost?" Noah jeered. "I don't believe you."

"It's true," Robbie said. "You're in my old bedroom. And my twin sister Beka is standing right behind you. She's a ghost, too."

Noah twirled, tripping over the chair. His gaze darted back and forth. "Are you r-really here?"

Suddenly, it occurred to Beka that she might be able to communicate with Noah, too, if she typed a message on the screen.

Could she still type? It'd been years since she'd played on her grandfather's Underwood type-writer in his office at the *Juniper Daily News*.

She'd gotten pretty good at it, although Grand-father had called her system "advanced hunt and peck."

Beka tried to move around Noah, accidentally slicing through his shoulder with her arm. She felt him shiver, even though he was already wearing his jacket.

Placing her fingers on the keyboard, she held them there, concentrating until she felt the keys move under her fingers — meaning, now she had power over them. Slowly she typed: yes i'm here.

Noah stared at the screen, then backed toward the wall, flattening himself against the window.

"Nifty!" Beka exclaimed. She'd broken through the barrier! From her world into his.

She typed: don't be afrade afrayd

afraid. "Drats, I'm a better speller than that."
She wondered how to erase the wrong words.

Noah's gaze followed the sound of the clicking
keys. He moved closer and gaped at the message
on the screen.

Beka added: we've lived here many years.
we won't hurt you.

Noah shoved hair away from his eyes. "This is
so-o-o-o cool," he said, but his voice sounded
unsure.

"Hey!" Robbie yelled. "I'm not sure how to
smoosh when there's nothing in front of me to
smoosh through. Raz, get us out of here."

"What's he talking about?" Noah turned to face
Beka, but sort of addressed the whole room since
he didn't know where she was.

Beka typed: can we brin my brother back
now? She never could find the *g* key, so she just
skipped it.

Robbie seemed jumpy, Beka noticed. As if he
thought the snow monster would rise up over the
hill again. She hoped the PAUSE button was holding back the monster.

Meanwhile Noah had erased the messages and
was studying the keys. With a "Why not?" type
of shrug, he held down the OPTION key and hit
RETURN at the same time.

The screen flickered. Static sparked across the

scene, as if a blizzard had just hit Killer Mountain. Then a gust of icy wind swirled through the room, depositing Robbie and Thatch in its wake.

The two sprawled on the floor.

"Headache?" Beka asked.

"No, thank you. I already have one." Robbie moaned. "I feel like I've been run over by the red skier."

"You would have been if Noah hit the wrong keys."

Noah was still tinkering with the computer.

"Hey, he doesn't know you're back." Beka reached for the keys and typed: you can stop now. they're here.

Noah grinned. "No kidding?" he said. "It worked?"

yep, Beka typed. It was supposed to be *yes*, but her finger slipped.

Noah read her message. "Wow," he said. "I have a couple of ghosts for friends." He sounded as though he was having a hard time believing his own words.

and a host do, too, Beka typed.

"What's *that* mean?" Robbie and Noah chimed together.

"It's ghost dog without the *g*'s," Beka explained. *Darn that key*, she added to herself.

Whether he got the message or not, Noah

35

danced around the room, excited by the prospect of communicating with ghosts.

All of a sudden his dance turned into limping, as if he suddenly thought of his bad leg — and remembered that people were watching.

Robbie and Beka exchanged glances.

"So? Is he faking an injured leg?" Beka asked. "To keep from facing Zip Boston in the junior ski race?"

"Why are you asking me?" Robbie gestured toward the keyboard. "Now's your chance to ask *him*."

7
Crashing and Burning

Beka's fingers hovered above the keys. "I'm trying to come up with a polite way to word my question," she explained to Robbie's quizzical look.

"Ready for dinner?" came a voice from the doorway.

Noah's mother leaned into the room. She'd changed into jeans and a cowboy shirt. Her hair was wet from the shower. White rings circled her eyes where the ski goggles had been.

"I didn't hear them come in," Robbie said.

"Me neither." Beka lifted her hands off the keyboard. Might not be the best time to type a list of questions on the screen.

Noah seemed flustered by the appearance of his

mother, as if he was trying to hide something in his room. Like two ghosts and a dog.

"Are you okay?" she asked.

"Sure."

Robbie thought he was acting way too guilty.

"Why are you wearing your jacket inside?"

He shrugged. "I got cold."

Instantly, she rushed to him, laying a hand on his forehead. "Are you getting sick?"

"No, Mom." He backed away from her hand. "How was the snow?"

"Perfect," his mother gushed. "Another layer is expected tonight. Conditions for tomorrow's race should be ideal." She cocked her head at him. "You would've had so much fun today. I saw some of your old racing buddies — Chip and his sister, Susie."

"Mmmmm," was Noah's answer.

"Well, I know you're probably starved by now. Give me time to dry my hair, then we'll go into Juniper for dinner." She started to leave. "Oh, Noah?"

"Yeah?"

"I'm sorry I mentioned the medallion today. It just slipped out."

"It's okay."

She left.

Noah closed the door. "I have to leave," he told the ghosts. "But first I want to find out why you're haunting this house." A slow grin spread across his face. "*And*, if I can hire you to haunt somebody for me."

"Uh-oh," Robbie said. "Suddenly we're ghosts for hire."

Beka laughed. "Not a bad idea. You snare 'em; we scare 'em."

Robbie groaned. He placed his hand on the computer screen. It felt warm, as if it were alive. He still hadn't gotten over the sensation of being inside the machine. "Come here, Sis, I want you to ask Noah a few questions."

"Why can't *you* ask him?"

"Because you can type. I can't. We'd be here all night while I searched for the letters in my own name."

She plunked down in the desk chair. "Should I answer his questions first?"

"Yeah. And ask him if Zip Boston is the one he wants us to haunt."

Beka typed the question. Fortunately there were no *g*'s.

Noah's eyebrows shot up. "How'd you know about her?"

we've been followin you.

"No kidding?"

"Tell us about the medallion," Robbie said, nudging his sister's arm.

She typed the question.

Noah sighed. He paced the room as if trying to come up with a reason to change the subject. "First, tell me where you are so I don't bump into you."

doesn't matter. you'd move riht throuh (rite thru) us. Beka was proud of her recovery on the *g* words.

"Yikes," Noah muttered. "What about the dog? Does he bite?"

only if you deserve it.

"Beka, stop," Robbie said. "He'll believe you."

"I'll sit at the desk so I can read your questions and answers." Noah moved cautiously across the room.

Beka jumped out of the way as he sat.

"The medallion," he repeated, tilting the chair back, ready to begin. "First of all, I'm one of the best ski racers in the country."

we know.

Noah let the chair clunk to the floor. "You know more about me than I thought." He tilted back again. "My parents make their living ski racing. I travel with them, keeping up with school on good ol' Mac here." He paused to pat the computer.

"He named his computer?" Beka said, wrinkling her nose.

"I started racing three years ago when I was eight," Noah continued. "Won a few medals, but not a gold one — never a first place. The race here at Walrus Mountain is important to me because this is where my dad won his first gold when he was my age."

Noah's eyes lit up. "It was a *cool* medallion — egg-shaped, with a walrus on it. Dad gave it a special place of honor in his trophy case. He used to let me play with the medal, but I wasn't allowed to take it out of the house."

Noah shifted uncomfortably, remembering. "Last year when we came here for the winter carnival, I knew my dad *really* wanted this to be my first big win, too. He wanted his son to take home the gold walrus medallion."

Robbie felt sympathetic. Noah had a lot of pressure on him to win.

"And Zip was here last year. She's good. I thought I needed all the help I could get, so I smuggled Dad's medal out of the trophy case and carried it with me. I thought if I wore it during the race, it'd bring me luck."

Noah gazed at the ceiling, as if the scene of last year's race was playing itself out like a movie. "Well, I crashed and burned. Missed a turn and skied off a hidden ledge, then smashed into a grove of evergreens. I got hurt. The ski patrol had to take me off the mountain on a stretcher."

"I'm sorry," Robbie said, although he knew Noah couldn't hear him.

"By the time we got to the hospital back home, and the painkiller wore off, I remembered the medallion. It must have flown off my neck when I crashed. Now it's lost in that grove of evergreens up on the mountain, buried under a season's worth of new snow."

He jumped to his feet, as though the memories were too painful to recall sitting still. "Dad never said anything. I guess he figured it out. But I was hurt badly enough that he was just glad to have me alive."

Noah threw a guilty glance around the room, as though afraid the word *alive* might offend the ghosts.

"After that, I went through months of physical therapy to regain the use of my legs. And it worked; I'm fine now — almost. But the thought of facing the top of the mountain again . . . um, well, it *scares* me."

what about zip? Beka typed.

"*She* doesn't scare me." Noah's voice sounded defensive.

Beka took a deep breath and typed the next line: i think she does.

"What? I'm not afraid of her. I could beat her with my eyes closed. I could beat her skiing without poles."

what about chip?

"Her brother? Ha. He'll never win first place. He skis out of control. That's how he got his nickname — Chip. He's crashed so many times, he's chipped off all his front teeth."

i think you ski inside your computer because you're afraid to face zip boston on the slopes. Beka was pleased that she got the word *afraid* right this time.

"Be-ka!" Robbie snapped. How could his sister be so mean?

Noah's face turned red as her words sunk in. Angry, he hit a few keys, then blanked the computer screen, shutting it down.

Grabbing his jacket, he flew out the door and around the landing, then stopped. Adding the limp to his walk, he awkwardly descended the stairs.

8
Disaster at Blaze's Burgers

"**H**ow could you say that to him?" Robbie felt annoyed that Beka had ended their conversation by making Noah mad. "He's the first person we've talked to in fifty years, and now he's not speaking to us."

"Sorry." Beka offered him a sheepish look. "But don't you agree? Don't you think he needs to ski that mountain again? And face Zip, too?"

"Doesn't matter whether I agree or not," Robbie scoffed. "It's up to Noah. You can't *make* him get up on that ski run tomorrow."

"*I'm* not," Beka said, going out the door. "*You* are."

"Me?" Robbie clicked his tongue at Thatch to

rouse him off the bed, then hurried after his sister. "What do you mean?"

"Hurry," was all she said. "Or we'll be late for dinner."

"Dinner?" Robbie mumbled. "What's the point of going to dinner with Noah if I can't talk to him?"

"You can learn a lot by listening."

Outside, the twins climbed into the Frenches' car seconds before the doors closed. "That was close," Beka said, trying to hold Thatch down.

Thatch loved going for rides in anything that moved. Beka finally let go of his collar. The dog immediately scrambled into the front seat for a better view — sitting on Mrs. French's lap. Sort of.

The sight was pretty funny. Robbie had to laugh. If only Noah's mom knew a fifty-year-old ghost dog shared her seat (and body), she might not be smiling and chatting with her husband the way she was. She *did* flip on the heat, though, so she must have felt the "ghost chill."

The group stopped at Blaze's Burgers for dinner. Blaze was one of the twins' favorite townspeople. She had bright-red hair and was always laughing. They'd known her grandmother — the original Blaze — who opened the café back in the forties.

"We can't let Thatch go inside a restaurant," Beka said, hesitating by the front door. "He'll be too hard to control."

"Think so?" Robbie scouted the area for anything that might lure the dog away. "I'd rather keep him with us."

"But remember how yummy Blaze's burgers and onions smell when they're sizzling on the grill?"

"Mmmm. Good point." The image made Robbie realize how long it had been since he'd bitten into one of those heavenly burgers. And the salty fries.

Beka ordered Thatch to sit by the door.

"Stay," they both told him.

Thatch whined, but obeyed. When the twins slipped through the door with other diners, the dog barked to let them know he didn't like being left behind.

Five people crowding around a circular booth was a tight fit. (Well, three people and two ghosts.)

Blaze was mopping the floor. She stopped for a minute to greet her newest customers. Then she returned to the bucket and mop while a waitress dressed in a red-and-white checked uniform that matched the tablecloth and curtains took everyone's order.

Robbie ordered an imaginary cheeseburger with invisible fries. Beka ordered ghost pancakes smothered with boo-berries — ha!

Mr. French began to rave about today's snow conditions on Walrus Mountain, and how *pumped* he was for tomorrow's races.

"Pumped?" Beka repeated. "Does he mean excited?"

Robbie shrugged. Keeping up with changes in language wasn't easy.

Mr. French finished his raving, then set a hand on Noah's arm. "There's still time for you to enter the junior race, Son."

Noah drew his arm away. "We've been through this already." He was saved from saying more by the arrival of the burgers.

"When did Dr. Faruka say you could hit the slopes again?" his mother asked.

"Soon."

"I'm glad she's making you do all those exercises to keep you in shape." Mrs. French sipped home-made lemonade — another one of Blaze's specialties. "Did you do your exercises today?"

Noah scrunched his face. "I forgot. I'll do them when we get home."

His dad did *not* look pleased. "If you didn't waste all your time glued to that computer, you — "

Mrs. French nudged him to hush. "Did you finish your article?"

"Um." Noah dipped a fry into a blob of catsup. "I'm working on it."

"You should be finished by now. What did you do all afternoon?"

Noah grinned, then tried to hide it. "I, um, played a few games, and — "

"Games," his father muttered.

Suddenly Noah straightened, as if it just occurred to him that the ghost twins could be sitting right here at the table with him. He peered at the empty spaces in the booth.

"What's wrong?" his mother asked.

"Do you believe in ghosts?" Noah's grin returned, as if he enjoyed keeping this little secret from his parents.

"Ghosts?" his father echoed. "What are you talking about?"

"Haunted houses and all that?"

Mr. French faced his wife. "What's gotten into him? Is he starting to believe his computer games are *real*?"

"I guess he has too much idle time," she answered. "We've got to get him back in training." She turned her attention to Noah. "When we get home, I'm calling Coach Monetta to tell her you're ready to resume training."

"But — "

Mr. French held up a hand, which, Robbie knew, in parent talk meant *end of discussion.*

"Boy, are *they* tough to please," Beka said.

Robbie was trying to decide if he could snitch a french fry off Noah's plate without anyone noticing, when his attention was suddenly drawn to the front door.

A man was holding it open while his wife stopped to pick up a newspaper. "Oh, no," Robbie whispered, jabbing Beka's ribs.

Thatch knew an opportunity when he saw one. He flew through the door at a dead run. The instant his paws hit the wet tile Blaze had just mopped, he skidded out of control across the floor.

Beka gasped.

Robbie held his breath. Thatch slid right through the legs of two waitresses, three tables, and one customer. But when he reached the bucket, he made solid contact.

The bucket went flying. Sudsy water sloshed across the floor. Customers screamed and jumped out of the way. A few grasped tables to keep from slipping.

"What happened?" Blaze hollered to a waiter behind the counter.

"The b-bucket fell over all b-by itself," he stammered in disbelief.

Robbie jumped from the booth, rushing toward Thatch, who'd come to a stop against the far wall. "Are you okay, boy?"

The dog seemed dazed.

Robbie never understood why Thatch could do things they couldn't. Like make the bucket move without concentrating on it first. Or *smoosh* into the computer — something they'd never *think* of trying. He often wondered if they *did* have the same powers, and just didn't know it.

Beka rushed to them, kneeling to check Thatch and make sure he was all right. Then she started to laugh at the chaos Thatch had caused.

"Sis, it's not funny." Robbie watched customers leave half-eaten meals and hurry to pay so they could get out of this weird place. Blaze mopped up the mess while trying to calm everyone.

The sight *was* funny, although Robbie felt sorry for Blaze. Thatch hadn't meant to scare away her customers. How could one innocent ghost dog cause so much commotion? The way he randomly made contact with the "real world" was a bit unnerving.

Robbie spotted Noah. He'd crept toward the now-empty bucket and was inspecting it.

"Look," Robbie said, pointing him out to Beka. "Now he knows we followed him. Think it will convince his parents to believe in us?"

"Ha," Beka said. "They think the ghosts Noah told them about are characters in one of his computer games."

Robbie grasped Thatch by the collar and led him toward the door. "Well, they're right," he told her. "We *are* characters in a computer game — *The Ghosts of Killer Mountain.* . . ."

9

Look Who's Talking

"**H**e's mad at us," Beka said in a quiet voice. "I wonder why?" Robbie couldn't keep sarcasm from his words.

They were sitting in Noah's room watching him fiddle with everything *except* the computer — as if he was avoiding turning it on.

Scattering his schoolbooks onto the bed, he stared at them.

"Great," Robbie muttered. "Now he's going to do his homework."

"Maybe we can help him?" Beka offered.

"Only if he's studying the 1940s." Robbie felt guilty snapping at his sister. She was just trying to smooth things over.

Suddenly Noah stepped to the door, listened

for a moment, then closed it. "So, are you ghost guys here?"

"Yes," Robbie answered. "But you'll never know unless you turn on the computer so we can talk to you."

"Wait," Beka said. She took hold of Noah's history book, concentrating on it until it shifted in her hand. As she picked it up, the book moved into the twins' dimension, becoming invisible to someone who might be watching.

Someone like Noah.

Gasping, he backed against the bureau.

Beka let go of the book. Falling to the bed, it sparked a green light as it moved back into the other dimension. Then it smacked against the other books and came to rest.

"Nice show, Raz," Robbie said.

"You *are* here," Noah exclaimed, then frowned. "I shouldn't even talk to you. It's just that . . . well, I'm curious about you. I want to know two things. First, did you have anything to do with what happened tonight at Blaze's Burgers? And second, why are you haunting this house?"

He paused, as if waiting for another physical sign from the ghosts.

"Turn on the computer and we'll tell you," Beka singsonged, taking her place next to the desk chair.

Noah turned on the computer, like he was obeying Beka's silent command. "Open new file," he said. "Name file: *Ghost*."

The file opened, giving Beka a whole screen to write on.

"Wow," she whispered. "We've got our own file." She rested her hands on the keys until they moved.

Robbie's curiosity made him inch closer to watch.

Thatch hopped onto the chair.

"Be nice, now," Robbie warned his sister. "Don't make Noah mad again."

Beka typed: why won't you ski in the race?

"No, no, no." Noah crossed his arms in rebellion. "I get to ask *you* questions now. You already learned about me." He plopped into the chair, making Thatch leap to the floor. "Am I sitting on anybody?"

not anymore.

Noah jumped up. "Maybe I should give *you* the chair," he said to Beka. "Since you'll be typing."

He moved to one side while Beka sat.

Noah leaned against the desk. "Okay, I'm waiting. Tell me your story."

Beka looked to Robbie for advice.

Robbie held Thatch out of the way. "Why don't you answer the questions he asked?"

Nodding, she typed: yes, we followed you to dinner. thatch knocked over the bucket. sorry.

Noah *hmmm'd*, as if Beka's words fit the explanation he'd worked out in his head.

as for us, this was our home fifty years ao. (More g trouble.) we came back as hosts.

"Hosts?" Noah read. "Ghost hosts? Ha!" he laughed at his own joke. "How'd you get to be ghosts?"

Beka pretended to collapse. "I can't believe he asked such a stupid question."

"Please don't type that; don't call him stupid." Robbie wished he could take over at the keyboard before his sister insulted Noah.

if you want to know our story, o to the juniper library and ask for the newspaper account about the zuffel twins.

Beka hurried on: now about you. we think you should ski in the race tomorrow.

Noah glanced away from the screen. "You sound like my mother."

robbie wants you to teach him how to ski.

"What?" Noah said. "How?"

Robbie read her message twice because it confused him. "Is this what you meant when you said *I'm* going to get Noah up on the mountain?"

She flashed him a big smile. "Watch and see." Then she typed: rob can stand on the back of your skis and hold on to your jacket. then you can show him what to do.

Noah scratched his head, wandering the room, thinking.

Suddenly his eyes grew wide. "I know," he exclaimed. "I *will* teach your brother how to ski. But not with me — with the red skier."

Robbie stared at him. "The red skier? You mean, you want me to go *back* into the computer and tag along with the robot skier?" He gestured at his sister. "Type that. Type what I just said."

"Noooo." She lifted her fingers off the keys. "That's too many words — and *g*'s."

"So what? Type it."

But it was too late. Noah waved Beka out of the chair and took over, calling up Killer Mountain on the screen. "This is a great idea," he said. Then, "Rob, where are you? Are you ready?"

"Go on, go on," Beka urged.

Robbie gaped at his sister. "Why are you so eager for me to go back in there?"

"Don't you see?" She looked at him as if her

meaning were clear as water. But to him, it was more like mud.

"See what?"

"If you can get Noah to help you *inside* the computer, maybe he'll let you help him *outside* the computer."

"Like on Walrus Mountain?"

Beka's giant grin was starting to annoy him. "Yes! After Killer Mountain, the race on Walrus will be a piece of cake."

Robbie sighed, giving in. He trudged toward the computer as if he were walking the plank on a pirate ship. "Piece of cake," he muttered. "Only if I *return* from Killer Mountain."

10
Robbie versus Killer Mountain

"Open *Killer Mountain*," Noah commanded.

The computer obeyed, churning briefly, then offering a list of options. "This is called the menu," he explained to the ghosts.

Noah twirled the ball on the keyboard that moved an arrow anywhere on the screen he wanted it to go. "This is a trackball," he added. "It works the same as a mouse."

a mouse? Beka typed.

Thatch began to bark. He knew what a mouse was.

"Forget it," Noah said.

Placing the arrow on the menu, he clicked a bar, choosing Red for the skier, Easy for the difficulty level, and Slow for the speed.

Then he pulled the chair away from the desk so Robbie could stand in front of the screen.

"How exactly does your brother get in there?" Noah asked.

Beka reached around Robbie to type: he smooshes while i keep hittin the key marked esc. She rested one finger on the key.

"Ha," Noah chuckled. "The escape key." He scratched his chin. "What does *smoosh* mean?"

lon story. tell you later.

"Did you grow up before the *g* was invented?" Noah teased.

ood joke, Beka typed.

Robbie prepared to *smoosh*, but his mind refused to cooperate. He worried about his earlier trip into the game, and how frightened he'd been. The whole situation was so far from reality, he hadn't known what to expect.

Of course, being a ghost was pretty far from reality, too, and he'd gotten used to that.

Robbie stood like a statue, remembering his first sensation on the inside. (After the headache.) The air around him had been terribly cold. Much colder than the air in Noah's room.

Good thing ghosts only *sensed* the cold and wetness, but didn't *feel* it, or he would have quickly frozen into a *ghost*sicle.

Robbie remembered Thatch's yelp of greeting,

59

and how the dog had rushed to make sure he was all right. Then Thatch had tried to get Robbie to follow him back to the game lady with the baby carriage. The lady who stood frozen, one leg forward midstep.

"She's not real, Thatch," he had said. "She's . . . she's like a robot." He remembered reading stories about robots back in the third grade.

Then Robbie remembered his anxiety about turning around. What would he see? The inside of a giant computer screen? Would he see Noah and Beka? With faces a million times larger than his?

His curiosity had mingled with apprehension as he'd pivoted. What he saw was . . . more snow, and the steep hill, angling down the mountain, bordered by evergreens. And a huge, cloudless blue sky.

"Wow," he'd whispered. "It's like I really *am* in another world."

That's when Beka's voice had come through loud and clear: "Robbie, say something out loud."

He'd grabbed Thatch by the collar, then waved and yelled, "Noah, can you hear me?"

"What's wrong?"

Noah's voice shattered his daydream, making him flinch.

"Rob, you're not concentrating hard enough," Beka said.

"Oh, sorry. I was . . . remembering what it was like before." He felt embarrassed that he'd been standing there like a zombie, staring at the screen. "I'm ready now."

As he regained his focus, something inside his chest began to flutter.

Thatch whined, as if he sensed Robbie's stress.

"Hold it." Robbie clicked his fingers, calling the dog to his side. "I need Thatch with me. For . . . well, I just need him with me."

"Fine," Beka said. "Should I tell Noah?"

"He'll figure it out when he sees Thatch on the screen."

"Is something wrong?" Noah asked again, still confused by the delay.

hold your horses, Beka typed.

Robbie wondered if people still used that expression. If not, Noah probably thought Beka was crazy.

Kneeling, he wrapped his arms around the dog. "Inside, Thatch," he whispered. "We're going inside."

Robbie focused, concentrated, strained until he

thought the headache was starting too early. He could tell by Beka's stillness beside him that she was mentally helping him.

Nothing happened.

"What's wrong?" she finally whispered.

"I think I know." The problem had been poking at the back of Robbie's mind. "We're focusing on the menu, not the game. Thatch doesn't understand what I want him to do. He needs a *reason* to go inside. Like someone to rescue."

"You're right." Beka rested her hands on the keys until she could type: start ame.

"Start game?" Noah translated. He stepped toward the computer. "Is everyone out of my way?"

"Gee, you'd think this guy never walked through ghosts before," Robbie teased, pulling Thatch aside.

Beka quickly explained their predicament.

"Start game," Noah commanded.

The computer beeped and blipped and blinked.

Suddenly the red skier whisked onto the chairlift, chugging up the mountain. Music began to play. The kind of music heard in scary movies.

One of Thatch's ears flew up. He was hooked.

"I've got a great idea." Noah tapped a key. "Open clip file," he said.

A rectangle opened in a corner of the screen,

offering Noah a menu. Scanning the list, he clicked "crying baby," then closed the file.

By this time the red skier was approaching the end of his ride on the chair. Noah twirled the ball until an arrow pointed at the top of the hill. When he clicked, the crying baby appeared as the skier came off the lift.

Thatch's other ear went up.

"Instant replay," Noah commanded. "Twenty times."

The baby wailed, and the skier came off the lift. Over and over and over.

Crying babies were a sight Thatch could *not* resist.

"*Grr-woof!*"

"Now he's ready." Robbie knelt in front of the screen, hanging onto his dog. "Inside, Thatch," he whispered. "The baby needs your help." Guilt tingled through Robbie over lying to his dog. *He* was the one who needed Thatch's help — not the robot baby.

Robbie held on tight, telling his own mind to go to Killer Mountain.

Familiar dizziness swept over him. Beneath his arms, Thatch trembled.

Pinpricks in the skin. Roaring in the ears. A sensation of tumbling through cotton candy.

Whomp!

Robbie spit out a mouthful of snow, sputtering, trying to catch his breath.

Thatch was belly-crawling up the hill toward the baby, as if he couldn't wait to recover first from *smooshing*.

Robbie chose to wait. Oh, the pain in his head.

Then it was gone as fast as it had come.

And so was the baby.

Noah must have cut the baby from the scene.

The skier stopped repeating his action, and sailed across the hilltop.

Robbie knew he didn't have much time to climb on board. Scrambling to his feet, he dusted snow off his clothes while trying to run through drifts so deep, it almost called for swimming.

Thatch was running in circles, searching for the missing baby.

"Thatch!" Robbie called. "Stay with me."

The red skier took the starting position. Robbie circled behind, then placed a foot on each ski, and grasped the figure's jacket. "Hello," he said in jest. "I'm Robbie Zuffel. I'll be traveling with you today."

Of course the robot-guy didn't know he had a stowaway.

Then they were off, flying down the mountain.

Thatch bounded through the drifts beside them, barking wildly.

Robbie caught his breath. If this was *Slow*, he wished Noah had clicked *Very, Very Slow*. This slow was too fast.

As the red skier carved his first turn and angled across the slope, Robbie held on with all his strength.

An instant later, something dark loomed further down the hill, right in the skier's path.

Robbie couldn't make out what it was. They were moving too fast.

And besides, his mind was way too busy trying to convince him that coming back to Killer Mountain wasn't a big, big mistake.

11
Wild Ride

Robbie ducked his head behind the red skier's back, afraid to watch.

But fear tapped him on the shoulder, telling him it might be smarter to stay alert to what was happening.

Then he remembered. Noah was controlling the skier. *He* was the one Robbie was hanging onto — not the red robot.

The skier cut through a drift, making a quick turn with a little jump. The jump scared Robbie. He grasped the figure around the waist.

The fact that he could even hold on to the skier startled him. The figure wasn't real, he kept reminding himself. That's why his arms wouldn't go through the skier like they would a live person.

Hanging on tight made it much easier to keep his balance.

Robbie peeked.

Then wished he hadn't.

The object at the bottom of the hill — the one they were barreling toward — was a . . . a kangaroo? Slow hop-hopping across the slope, her tail making swirls in the snow. A kangaroo baby, sitting tall in its mother's pouch, appeared to be reading a book.

The bizarre sight made Robbie laugh. Kangaroos on a ski slope? Reading?

Thatch zipped ahead. His warning bark was loud enough to wake the zombie robots.

Robbie wasn't sure Thatch knew what a kangaroo was. Not many of them hopped around the Kickingbird Lake Resort.

But that didn't stop Thatch. The dog lunged at the kangaroo.

Robbie held his breath.

Seconds before the skier bent his knees to jump the animals, the kangaroo and her baby toppled over in the snow, like ducks in the shooting gallery at the carnival.

The skier wobbled. Or was it Noah who wavered — to keep the skier from smashing into Thatch?

Either way, it sent the robot — and Robbie —

slicing through the snow at breakneck speed. On their faces. Eating lots of cold wet snow.

Robbie floundered through deep powder, missing an outcropping of rocks by inches. Since he'd made solid contact with the skier, logic told him he'd make solid contact with everything in the game, including rocks and kangaroos. Ouch!

Thatch was at his side in seconds.

"Hey!" Robbie winced. "Licking my face is *not* going to help." Back on his feet, he surveyed the hill. The game was still in progress. Music played. The kangaroo continued leaping, only she didn't go anywhere — just wiggled in place on her side.

Robbie gave Thatch's neck a good rubbing. "Sorry I snapped. But you're here to *help* me, not cause me to turn into a ghost cannonball."

As he plowed through drifts, he turned in a circle, making sure nothing was coming at him. "Let's go help Mr. Red."

The skier was still face down in the snow. Noah was probably waiting to see if Robbie was all right before he sent the figure off again with his passenger.

"Are you okay?" came Noah's voice as if he'd read Robbie's mind.

Robbie waved both arms in the air to show he was fine.

Instantly the red skier came to life — so to speak.

Robbie groaned before climbing onto the skis. "Why am I doing this again? Beka had better be right — "

Then they were off. Facing more obstacles: a boy wearing knickers, tending a herd of goats; a table surrounded by cowboys playing poker; a horse taking a bubble bath in an old-fashioned tub; and sweethearts paddling a canoe across the slope.

Noah was good. And quick. And smart. He kept the skier positioned right in front of Thatch, so the dog couldn't see what was coming up. That way, they cleared each obstacle before Thatch had a chance to react.

"Brilliant, Noah!" Robbie called, wondering if the boy could hear him.

Then Noah messed up.

Thatch changed course without warning, breaking away from the skier's path. It wouldn't have been so bad, if it wasn't for the next obstacle.

Frilly-dressed ladies at a fancy table sipped tea from pink china cups. The *problem* was that all the ladies at the tea party happened to be — cats!

Thatch went berserk.

And it wasn't because he planned on saving anybody.

No matter what world or dimension Thatch was in, cats were cats and dogs were dogs. Cats were born to be chased by dogs, whether they wore frilly dresses and sipped tea or not.

Robbie tried to shout a warning to Noah, but the words froze on his tongue.

Thatch raced toward the cat party, took a flying leap, and landed in the middle of the table. Cups and saucers flew off into the snow. Everything went flying — except the cats.

"They're not real!" Robbie shouted, even though he knew Thatch wouldn't understand.

The cats continued their party unaware that the table's crystal centerpiece had been replaced by a shaggy centerpiece that growled.

Thatch was confused. Cats *never* ignored him. Ever.

Snarling, he bared his teeth. Not a good sign.

Noah must have been figuring out what to do because he relaxed control of the skier.

"Look out!" came Beka's voice.

The skier smashed into the table, sending the cats and Thatch plopping into the surrounding drifts.

Robbie sailed over the table, landed hard, then rolled through the snow — first on top of Thatch, then underneath.

They came to a rest against the bare trunk of an oak tree.

"Skiing is not as much fun as I thought it would be," Robbie mumbled.

Thatch scrambled to his feet, peering back toward the upturned table, as if his dog pride was trying to figure out why the cats ignored him.

Suddenly Noah's voice broke the quiet. "Oh, no, I should have seen him coming."

The words brought Robbie to his feet. He'd heard that line before. That's what Noah had said right before the blue skier was eaten by . . .

A dark form loomed over the tall tops of a juniper grove.

"The snow monster!" Robbie yelled.

12
The Snow Monster

Grabbing Thatch's collar, Robbie scuttled behind the oak, then realized it wasn't wide enough to hide them both.

In a panic, he scouted the area, hurrying Thatch behind a snow-covered boulder that looked like a giant marshmallow.

Perfect.

Every muscle in Thatch's body was tensed. It was all Robbie could do to keep him from bolting toward the towering monster, who, upon surveying his next feast, was now growling even louder than the dog.

The monster moved toward the ruined tea party. Picking the cats up one by one, he popped them into his mouth.

Seeing the cats' demise must have pleased Thatch, but it quickly turned Robbie's legs to rubber.

The skier, still laying in the snow, moved in jerky motions, yet didn't go anywhere. Robbie figured Noah was trying to rescue him.

Rescue *him*? Robbie turned to face the wide blue sky, where he assumed the computer screen was. "What about *me*?" He tried to yell the words, but fear turned them to mush.

Huddling behind the boulder, he held on to Thatch for comfort.

One of the dog's ears was crooked upward, as if he couldn't quite figure out what the beast was. A gigantic dog? A bear? He'd seen a few bears in the woods around Kickingbird Lake.

Thatch stopped trying to tear away from Robbie's grasp. *The monster's size must be intimidating him*, Robbie thought. And not many things intimidated the ghost dog.

Robbie watched transfixed as the snow monster polished off the last cat and reached for the skier, who almost looked as if he were trembling from fear, instead of from Noah's quick movements on the keys.

Was the computer game malfunctioning?

"No, please," Robbie whispered. "Not now."

In one swift movement, the red skier became

history. Gone without a trace. A satisfied grin spread across the monster's ugly face. Out of his fanged mouth popped the skis and poles. Then he rubbed his huge, hairy tummy, growl-laughing.

The sight was one Robbie would rather watch while sitting on the floor in Noah's room — not this close. Not when he was probably the next victim.

"Noah!" Robbie screamed. At least he *tried* to scream. He doubted Noah could hear his frantic whisper. "Get me out of here. Why aren't you helping me?"

"Raz!" came Beka's voice.

She sounded scared. But not as scared as *he* was right now.

"You've got to *smoosh* back. We can't get the *return* key to work."

Robbie groaned. How was he supposed to concentrate with King Kong breathing down his neck?

Twirling, he faced Thatch toward the wild blue yonder. "*Think*, Thatch."

Then he remembered. The dog needed a reason to *smoosh*.

Robbie's brain whirred, searching for a way to give Thatch motivation. "Home, Thatch. To Beka. Find Beka."

Thatch's ears perked.

"Hurry, Rob!"

Beka's frightened voice did the trick. Thatch began to whine.

"Sis!" Robbie shouted. "Keep talking and Thatch will come to you." Could she hear him?

"Puppy!" Beka called. "Help me. Come here, Thatch, I need you!"

Good, Robbie thought. *Now it's my turn.* He focused on the blueness of the sky.

Then he made a big mistake.

He peeked around the boulder.

The snow monster was making his way across the slope, head raised, sniffing the air. He knew dessert lay nearby.

Robbie pie with Thatch à la mode.

Panicked, he forced himself to face the sky. Thatch began to tremble. At first Robbie thought his dog had seen the monster edging closer. Then a gust of icy wind smacked his face and Thatch was gone.

The dog had *smooshed* without him!

"Get out of there!" Noah and Beka yelled in one voice.

"Don't look back; don't look back," Robbie mumbled.

He stared at the sky, holding his hands over his ears so he couldn't hear the monster's sniffle-snorting as it drew closer. Robbie pretended the sky was the bed with the navy-blue quilt in Noah's room. His old bedroom.

Focus. Concentrate. Think!

Behind him snow crunched under giant clawed paws.

Beka. Picture Beka's face. "I'm coming home," he whispered.

Gr-r-r-r-o-o-o-o-o-wl!

Robbie jumped out of his skin and back in again. *Stay focused.*

"Beka, help me!" he screamed. He wished his sister would call him home the way she'd called Thatch.

"Robert Adam Zuffel!" she hollered, as if she'd read his mind, like twins do sometimes. "Come home! Hurry, Raz! Thatch and I need you!"

Fear swooped dizziness from his head to his toes.

Gr-r-r-r-o-o-o-o-o-wl!

The roar was so close, it deafened him.

Monster claws pricked his skin.

Then a blizzard kicked up, swirling snow, blinding him.

A giant hairy hand curled around him.

He remembered no more.

13
U O ME 1

Robbie held his breath, waiting for the monster's teeth to crush his bones. Instead, an opened closet door bumped his head as he sprawled on the floor of Noah's room.

Beka stood over him.

Noah still peered at the computer screen, his face as pale as Beka's. "What happened?" he muttered. "I can't see him with all this static."

"My brother is back," Beka blurted, then gave Robbie a sheepish grin. "I forgot. He can't hear me."

"*Woof?*" Thatch's bark sounded like a question, as if he couldn't believe his master had survived Killer Mountain and its snow monster.

"Good evening," Robbie groaned. "Thanks for

getting me out of there with no seconds to spare."

"We *tried*," Beka told him, sounding defensive. "The game malfunctioned. Thatch threw off the system when he interfered with the cat scene."

Robbie held his head and moaned a bit longer than he needed to, but he wanted Beka to feel good and sorry for him. "And you thought it was such a great idea for me to go into the game again."

She avoided his eyes. "Well, it *was* exciting."

"From *your* point of view. From mine, terrifying is a better word."

Noah was still at the computer, frantically typing commands and yelling at the screen.

"Go tell him I'm back. We're upsetting him for nothing."

They moved to the computer. Beka typed: he's back.

Noah flipped around in his chair, as if he expected to see Robbie standing behind him. Robbie *was* standing behind him, but Noah couldn't see him, of course.

Noah heaved a sigh of relief, then looked concerned. "Is Robbie okay? Is he . . . alive?"

nope, he's still dead.

Noah grimaced. "Sorry. I keep forgetting. Having ghost friends is weird."

"Let me talk to him." Robbie impatiently nudged Beka out of the way.

"But you can't type."

"Didn't stop you."

She gave him a playful smack. "Let's see if *you* can find the *g* key."

Robbie squinted at the keyboard. As soon as the keys yielded to his touch, he typed:

ggggggggggggggggggggggggggggggggg
ggggggggggg!!!!!

"Smart aleck," Beka snipped.

Noah frowned at the *g*s. "What does *that* mean?"

ROBIEE HEAR.

"You spelled both words wrong," Noah told him.

"I know. I did it on purpose."

"Right," Beka said, laughing.

U O ME 1, Robbie typed.

"Are we speaking in a secret code now?" Noah sat up straight, acting interested in this new game they were playing.

ITS NO KOD. I KANT TIPE.

"You can't spell, either." Noah threw a smug look in the direction of the ghost typist.

"I can spell fine, but not when I have to search for every letter." Robbie backed away from the keyboard. "Tell him I'm not going to talk to him if he keeps insulting me."

"Tell him yourself. You wanted to take over the keyboard." Beka climbed onto the bed to cuddle against a snoozing Thatch.

"I owe you one?" Noah read, figuring out the *code*. "What do you mean?"

Robbie placed his fingers on the keys once more: I SKEED KILLER MOUNTIN WITH THE REDD SKEER. YUR NEXT.

"You want *me* to go into the game?" Noah gasped each word.

NO, Robbie typed, although the idea intrigued him. Yet there was no way a human could *smoosh* like a ghost. I WANT TO SKEE WITH YOU ON WAL- RUS MOUNTIN.

Noah's eyebrows shot up. "Me? When?"

Robbie sensed both fear and excitement in Noah's voice.

2 MOROW. AT THE JR SKEE RACE.

"But — "

YUR AN XPERT. YU WER GRATE WITH THE RED SKEER. YOU CAN DO IT FOR REEL. ON WALRUS.

Noah jumped from the chair and strode across the room, mumbling to himself.

Robbie stepped close to listen. Even Beka came off the bed to catch what Noah was saying: "She's had the whole year to practice. Well, I have, too.

But only on computer — not on the slopes. I've stayed in shape, though, thanks to Dr. Faruka. . . ."

"I think he's arguing with himself," Beka said.

"You're right. But as long as he's away from the computer, I can't argue back."

Frustrated, Noah paced between the window and the closet. "I won't do it. I can't."

Beka tailed him, chanting, "You *can* do it. You can face the mountain. You can beat Zip Boston. You're fast. You're good. You've done it a million times in your mind. And your injury is healed. You can; you can; you can!"

"*Maybe* I can," Noah muttered, as though Beka's words filtered through his skull. "Maybe once I get up there, it won't seem so — "

The door swung open. Mrs. French, in her bathrobe, gaped at Noah as if she'd forgotten he was in there. "Who are you talking to?" Her gaze darted about the room.

"Ghosts?" Noah offered.

She shook her head, *tsking* at him. "It's late. You should be in bed. Our race is first up in the morning, so we need to get some sleep. You're making an awful lot of noise in here."

"Sorry, Mom."

She didn't leave. "Seriously, Son, who were you talking to?"

"Um, well, I'm practicing for . . . for a play. We're having tryouts when I get back to school."

"Oh, wonderful. A play. What's it called?"

Noah shrugged.

"If he's going to fudge to his mother," Beka groaned, "he shouldn't stand there looking so darn guilty."

"How can you practice lines if you don't know what play it is?"

"Um, we're making it up," he said. "We're writing the play."

"Wonderful."

"And we might call it *Ghost Racers*."

His mom's smile faded. "Oh, Noah, you play those games too much. If only . . ." Her voice trailed off. "Well, good night. Wish me luck for the race."

"Break a leg," he said cheerfully, then stopped. "Whoops. That's what you say when you're in a play — not in a ski race."

Fortunately, Mrs. French laughed.

"Good luck, Mom."

"And good night." She closed the door.

"Whew," Noah said. "You guys are getting me into trouble." Hurrying to the computer, he clicked it off without giving them a chance to answer.

"Good night, ghosts," he whispered, shoving off

his shoes and climbing into bed, clothes and all. "Go to your room, or wherever you go at night. I need time to think."

"How can we leave when the door is closed?" Beka kicked it to make her point.

"We can't," Robbie said. "Unless you want to *smoosh* through the keyhole."

"I've got a better idea." Beka settled into a chair beside the bed. Thatch stretched out next to Noah. "Story time," she singsonged.

Robbie sat backwards in the desk chair to listen.

"Once upon a time," Beka began, "a ski racer named Noah French faced the biggest challenge of his life. A challenge called Walrus Mountain."

Then Beka spent half the night convincing a sleeping Noah that he could whip Walrus Mountain — and Zip Boston, too.

14
Beka's Midnight Message

The morning dawned bright. Cold sunshine sparkled on three inches of freshly fallen powder. A perfect day for ski racing.

Robbie had watched the sun come up from his place at the bedroom window. He'd tried to close his eyes during the night and let his mind *float* the way ghosts do instead of sleeping.

But visions of snow monsters, with three evil eyes, pointy fangs, and sharp claws kept his eyelids flying open.

Even now in the glow of early dawn, the memory made him shiver.

He glanced at Beka. After midnight, she'd given up telling stories to Noah, and spent the rest of the time reading his schoolbooks.

"This is amazing," she said, poring over Noah's arithmetic book. "We never learned anything like this. It's called new math."

Robbie stretched and yawned. "What was wrong with the old math?"

"I don't know," she answered. "And you should read his history book. You wouldn't *believe* the things that have happened the last fifty years."

Noah woke up and rolled over — right through Thatch.

Thatch yipped, as if hurt, only Robbie knew he wasn't. The sensation was just an eerie one for a ghost.

Sitting up, Noah climbed out of bed, smoothing down his hair and stretching. "Are you ghost guys here this morning?"

The twins didn't answer. They couldn't unless he turned on the computer.

"Well if you *are* here," Noah began, pulling on his shoes, "the strangest thing happened last night." He sat at the desk and clicked on the computer. "I kept having weird dreams. I dreamed I was in the race today, and . . . and I was *amazing*. I made the run over and over, until I could picture the entire course in my mind. I even beat — "

He stopped, acting flustered, then gave his attention to the keyboard, opening the *Ghost* file on screen.

"And, you know what?" Noah continued. "Dream or no dream, I'm going to do it. I'm going to race today."

He chuckled, as if proud of his decision. "I know it sounds crazy. I haven't skied for a whole year. But I go to physical therapy four times a week, and Dr. Faruka makes me work hard. *Really* hard."

He twirled in the chair. "Robbie? Tell me if you're here. I have to ask you an important question."

Robbie stepped to the computer and rested his fingers on the keys until he had control over them. IM HERE.

"Great," Noah said. "Will you go to the race with me?"

SUR. IF U WANT ME 2.

"You can ride on the back of my skis, the way you did in the game."

Robbie's stomach flip-flopped. The memory of the red skier disappearing between the snow monster's fangs made him never want to go *near* a ski slope again. *But it's only a game,* his mind argued. *The skier wasn't eaten, and the monster doesn't exist.*

Still, he wondered if dangers on the *real* mountain might be worse than those in the game.

"Well?" Noah waited for an answer. "Will you ride with me?"

The idea fascinated him. Yet there was one problem. Reaching for the keys, he typed: I WONT BEE ABEL TO TALK TO U.

"Oh, yeah, I forgot." Noah combed his hair with his fingers. "But *I'll* be able to talk to *you*. And I'll feel a whole lot better if you're there because I would never have considered doing this if it hadn't been for you and Beka — and Thatch. Thatch has to come, too."

"Thatch? At a ski race?" Beka bit her lip. "Is he sure?"

Robbie gave her a determined "Yes." He'd already decided to take Thatch. Nothing seemed impossible when his faithful dog was by his side.

"Hey." Beka grabbed his arm, the way she did sometimes when she was having a brainstorm. "*I* know how you can talk to Noah. Sort of."

"What do you mean? Take the computer along?"

He'd meant it as a joke, but she looked at him as if he were crazy. "Do what I did last night," she said. "Talk to him and repeat your words. They sink in. He got the message, didn't he? The words Noah said when he woke up were the same ones I put into his brain while he was sleeping."

Robbie wasn't convinced.

"Just try it," she told him.

Noah yanked back his sleeve to look at his watch. "We've got to hustle. I have to register for the race and get my number."

Diving into the closet, he tossed out gloves, hats, goggles, boots, and a ski outfit (matching pants and jacket in shades of red, white, and blue).

When his head emerged from the closet, he said, "Is Beka here?" Moving to the computer, he waited for an answer.

yes, she typed.

"Um." Noah looked flustered. "Could you leave the room while I change clothes?"

Beka snickered. Last night, she'd suspected he'd slept in his clothes because he was too embarrassed to change in front of her.

She typed: first a question. where should i o to watch you race?

Noah read her words. "The best place to see everything is right here."

"Here?" Beka repeated. "Is he crazy?"

"My parents are racing right now. They always return to watch the other events on TV. You can watch with them."

"Great!" Beka loved watching TV, mainly because it hadn't been invented when she and Robbie were growing up.

"Tell him you're leaving the room," Robbie urged. "He's in a hurry."

i'll leave now if you open the door.

Noah opened the door, waited a few beats, then closed it and changed into his racing clothes.

Robbie paced the room. Part of him wished he could stay here with his sister and watch the whole thing on TV.

Yet another part of him *wanted* to take "wild ride number two."

Thatch's whining and dancing caught Robbie's attention. The dog was *not* sharing his apprehension. Obviously, Thatch was itching for more adventures on the mountain.

Robbie wondered if Thatch knew it would all be *real* this time.

15
Don't Look Down

Two boys and a dog hurried up Aspen Lane. To anyone watching, there was only *one* boy and no dog.

Noah struggled to move fast in his clunky ski boots, while balancing skis and poles over one shoulder. There was no sign of a limp.

Robbie wished he could offer his help. If he took hold of the skis until they moved under his power, he could lift them off Noah's shoulder and carry them.

But by doing so, the skis would become invisible. The disappearing act might not startle Noah, but it would certainly startle the pathway full of tourists and townspeople off to enjoy today's events at the winter carnival.

Thatch was beside himself, eyes and ears alert to the hustle and bustle around him.

Robbie felt the same way. Anticipation hung in the air like the fog descending over the hills around them, dimming this morning's brightness.

They hurried under the Moosehead entry arch, and zigzagged through the lodge area to the base of the mountain. Along the way were carnival booths and amusement park rides brought in for the special occasion.

A redheaded clown in a ski outfit handed a balloon to Noah, but he didn't take it. Robbie wished *he* could have it. Maybe on the way back, he could snitch one for Beka.

At the base of the mountain, they stopped at a table strung with a banner: ALL SKI RACERS REGISTER HERE.

Noah stepped up to the table and started to give his name to a lady wearing sunglasses that reflected like two tiny mirrors. Her nose was covered with cream as white as her hair.

Robbie thought she looked silly. Out of curiosity, he stepped between Noah and the lady to see if his reflection showed in her glasses. He saw Noah's reflection instead. *Makes sense*, he told himself.

"Noah French!" the lady exclaimed. "I know

who you are. The Walrus Mountain hot dogger of all time."

Noah gave a modest shrug.

"I didn't know you were racing this year," she said. "After your . . . uh . . . after what happened last year." Her voice trailed off, as though she was sorry she'd said so much.

"I changed my mind." Noah thrust his chin forward, looking proud. Then his expression changed to concern. "Am I too late to register? No one else is in line."

She glanced at her watch. "Oh, my, you'd better hustle. Here's your number." She thrust a folded piece of material at him. "Run and get on the lift. I'll do the paperwork for you, and notify the starter that one more racer is on his way."

Noah grabbed his number and hurried toward the base of the lift. "Rob," he whispered, so no one would think he was talking to himself, "stand beside me, and sit on the chair as soon as it hits the back of your legs."

Robbie followed, feeling unsure about the swinging chairs swooshing up the hill. Yet something told him the ride on the chair lift might be the *easiest* ride he took all day. "What about Thatch?"

"Can you hold Thatch on your lap?" Noah blurted, as if sensing Robbie's question.

"You've got to be kidding," was all Robbie had time to say. Grabbing Thatch's collar, he imitated Noah's quick movements, getting into place to catch the chair. Lifting Thatch took all his strength.

The chair hit his legs. He sat. Thatch scrambled to stay onboard, draping himself across both boys. Since his body went through Noah's, he curled his paws around the seat of the chair.

"Thatch is way too big for one lap," Robbie explained to Noah. "This is a *two*-lap dog."

"Gosh it's cold all of a sudden," Noah said. "But I guess it won't matter once I start skiing."

"It's cold because you have a ghost dog on top of you," Robbie told him. "And a scared one at that."

He held tight to the dog, whose worried gaze kept moving between his master's face and the ground, which was dropping further and further away.

Robbie, himself, was trying not to look at the disappearing earth.

"Don't look down," Noah warned. "It's kind of scary being up this high with nothing to hold you in the chair."

"You're a great mind reader," Robbie mumbled.

Poor Thatch. His forlorn eyes gazed at Robbie as if wondering if his master had lost his mind.

But Thatch's trust kept the dog still — except for a nervous whine that sounded almost as if he were crying.

"We're almost there," Noah said.

"We're almost there, Puppy," Robbie echoed, borrowing Beka's pet name. Comforting Thatch took his mind off his own fear of heights.

"At the top," Noah began, "I'll ski off to the left. You lean forward. And, when your feet touch the ground, jump off and run to the right to stay clear of the other chairs. Then come around the lift machinery to the starting line. I'll be taking my position. Climb onto the back of my skis, like you did in the game. And hold on tight. Thatch should be fine on his own."

Robbie sighed. "Sounds easy." He wondered why his brain didn't agree with his words. A zillion questions begged to be asked. Too bad he couldn't ask any of them.

Noah scooted forward on the chair and grasped his poles, ready to shove off.

Robbie felt Thatch quiver as they approached the top. Was he eager to get all four paws on land again? Well, so was Robbie. Two feet, that is.

At the ramp, Noah whooshed away.

Robbie jumped, as instructed, setting Thatch down as he ran. At least that's what he *tried* to do. What really happened was his shoes hit the icy ramp, making him exit on his bottom. Thatch, on his rump.

They landed in a snowdrift at the bottom of a short hill.

"No time to waste," Robbie said, coming to his feet. Grasping Thatch's collar, he hurried around the machinery.

A row of skiers was poised at the starting line. Noah was easy to spot. He was pulling on the cloth top the white-nosed lady had given him. Fitting like a sleeveless T-shirt, it read: WALRUS MOUNTAIN WINTER CARNIVAL. Under that was a large number 31.

"Thatch," Robbie ordered. "Stay with me." Quickly he ran toward Noah and climbed onto the back of his skis. He started to hang on tight, like Noah had told him, but his arms went right through the boy.

"I forgot," Robbie mumbled. He'd have to hang on to Noah's jacket, and hope for the best. "I'm here," he said to the back of Noah's head. "In case you're wondering."

Noah turned his head both ways. Robbie assumed he *was* wondering.

"Hey, Grindelwald!" came a sarcastic voice from down the line.

Noah and Robbie leaned forward to look.

Zip Boston smiled back. Her hot-pink ski outfit

was hard on the eyes, Robbie thought.

"What are *you* doing here?" she jeered.

Robbie heard Noah groan, but before he had a chance to answer, the starter yelled for everyone's attention.

"Skiers take your starting position," he hollered through a megaphone.

The skiers hunched over in unison, staring down the slope, poles in position to shove off.

"Ready!" the starter called.

Robbie heard Thatch whine. Or had that feeble cry come from *him*?

A gunshot echoed down the valley.

Then they were off, with Thatch racing madly behind.

And Robbie hanging on for dear life — which was an odd thought for a ghost to have.

16
The Race

Robbie tried hard to keep his eyes open, but every time he peeked around Noah's head to see where they were going, horror streaked through his veins like lightning.

It was easier to duck his head and hang on tight. He even tried whistling "Yankee Doodle Dandy" just to take his mind off his terror.

Oh yeah, he was supposed to be *helping* Noah, encouraging him. Robbie didn't think the guy needed encouragement, yet that's why he'd come along for the ride.

"You're doing great!" he yelled.

Then he dared a look to see if Noah *was*, in fact, doing anything worth shouting about.

Noah was leading the pack.

"Hey, you really *are* doing great!" Suddenly Robbie's fear became excitement. Noah was winning! He was doing it! The gold walrus medallion would have his name on it after all.

Robbie leaned around Noah and grinned into the wind, whooshing past so fast it took his breath away.

The sun broke through the clouds as if it shared Robbie's bright outlook.

Noah cut and sliced his skis back and forth across the slope, even faster than the blue skier on Killer Mountain's *Fast* mode.

Now it was easy to yell encouraging words into Noah's ear: "Keep it up! You're winning! You're the best! The hot dogger of Walrus Mountain!"

Where was Thatch?

Ah, there he was, racing and sliding on the hard packed snow, trying to keep up with them.

"We're gonna win, Thatch!" Robbie yelled.

Without warning, a shadow darkened the snow beside them. Someone was creeping up on Noah's lead.

Robbie immediately thought of the snow monster. Then he remembered that this wasn't a game.

Sucking in his breath, he twisted his head to look.

What he saw was *worse* than the snow monster.

What he saw was Zip Boston.

17

Number 31,
Who Are You?

Beka sat in the family room reading stories in Noah's Language Arts book until his parents came home from their race.

They'd both won their events.

Beka was impressed.

With pride, Mr. French placed two trophies on the fireplace mantel, then he and his wife toasted each other with glasses of orange juice.

"I only wish I could place one more prize on the mantel today," Mr. French said sadly.

His wife gave him a sympathetic look, then clicked on the TV. "Do you think Noah will come downstairs and watch the junior race?"

Mr. French finished his juice. "I'll go see if I can tear him away from his computer." Pulling off heavy boots, he padded upstairs in his socks.

"He's not in his room," Beka said, pointing at the TV. "He's there." She moved close to the screen, taking the book with her so it would remain invisible.

Cameras were trained on the starting line. One of the skiers was pulling something over his head. A T-shirt with a number on it. **31**.

Was it Noah?

Yes! Beka knew because Robbie was getting into position behind him. Ha, she could see the double skiers, but no one else could.

Where was Thatch? she wondered. *Out of camera range?*

"Hurry!" Mrs. French called. "They're getting ready to start." She pulled off her boots, too, and relaxed on the sofa.

"Starting lineup," the announcer was saying. Then he began to read off the names of the racers.

"He's not upstairs," Mr. French said, hurrying into the room, a worried look on his face.

"Told ya," Beka snipped.

Mrs. French didn't seem bothered by Noah's absence. "He probably went up to the carnival booths. And I'm glad he did," she added. "He needs more fresh air and exercise. To strengthen his leg."

Mr. French inhaled sharply. "Did you hear that?"

"What?"

Sinking onto the couch, he stared at the TV screen. "I swear they just announced Noah's name."

She patted his leg. "Honey, don't — "

A gun fired. The skiers were off.

Both Frenches leaned toward the screen. "Look at number thirty-one," Noah's mother gasped. "It *does* look like Noah's jacket."

Both were quiet as the skiers flew down the slope, zigzagging as fast as skiers in the computer game, Beka thought.

"In the lead," came the announcer's voice, "number thirty-one, Noah French."

"Yes!" Beka shouted.

"What?" Mr. French cried.

Mrs. French placed a hand on each cheek, as if overcome by the news.

"Running a strong second," the announcer continued, "is crowd favorite, number fifteen, Susie Boston, better known as — "

"Zip," Beka finished, snarling at the screen.

18
The Pink Vulture

Robbie gaped at the hot-pink streak that was Zip Boston.

She was moving so fast, her skis barely touched the ground. It almost looked as if she were flying down the slope. Like a pink vulture.

She inched closer and closer until she and Noah were skiing neck and neck. At a speed so fast, Robbie hated to think what might happen if either one of them slipped. Or crashed and burned, as Noah called it.

Then Noah noticed her. His arch rival. Slowly taking away his lead.

Robbie sensed a jolt through Noah, yet he didn't miss a beat.

"Come on. Come on!" Robbie yelled. "Ignore

her. You can do it. Think of the gold medallion."

Yes, Robbie added to himself. *Keep reminding Noah of the medal he wants so dearly to win.*

"Gold. Gold. Gold," he shouted into Noah's ear. "The gold medallion. The walrus. Think gold. Think medallion. Think walrus." Robbie chanted the words over and over.

In a heartbeat, Zip was ahead. Robbie didn't know how she did it, but suddenly he was staring at the back of her pink hat.

Noah tensed, leaning forward, straining to catch up.

Then it happened.

Zip caught an edge on an icy ridge. She swerved one way, then another, fighting to keep control.

She wobbled and wavered. Tottered and swayed.

Then she recovered.

But now she was behind. Way behind.

"We're ahead!" Robbie yelped. "The slope's all ours. She'll never catch us now."

Victory tasted as sweet as his memory of Blaze's sugary lemonade. Robbie licked his lips.

Then something went wrong.

Noah began to slow. The movement was slight, but he definitely was slowing.

"What are you doing?" Robbie screamed.

Noah took a sharp curve. Expertly. Then whipped across the slope.

Robbie leaned in for the turn. But the turn never came.

Noah skied straight ahead, off the trail, over a jump, and headed right for a grove of evergreens.

An unexpected mogul threw Noah off balance.

The last thing Robbie remembered was flying through the air — with frantic sounds of Thatch's barking ringing in his ears.

19
Not Again!

Now the Frenches were on their knees in front of the TV.

"Go, Son, go!" shouted Noah's father.

"My baby!" his mother cried. "I'm so proud of you."

"Your *baby*?" Beka hoped she didn't call Noah that in public.

Meanwhile, Beka was yelling for both boys. "Go, Noah! Hang on, Raz!" Every few moments, she'd catch a glimpse of Thatch. *Him* she wasn't worried about. He looked like he was having the time of his . . . well, he looked like he was having fun.

"Oh, no!" yelped Mrs. French.

"What?" Beka scrunched between them. "Oh, no," she repeated.

Zip was no longer tied with Noah.

"She's taken the lead!" Mr. French shouted. "Hang in there, Son. Don't let her beat you. That medal belongs to the French fam — "

"She caught an edge!" Mrs. French cried. "She's falling behind. Noah's got the lead again. Way to go!" Noah's mom was waving her arms like a cheerleader.

"Hold it steady, Son, don't — "

"Watch out!" Mrs. French covered both eyes. "What happened?"

"He skied off camera?" Beka offered.

Noah's mom peeked between her fingers while Mr. French and Beka stayed glued to the screen, waiting for another glimpse of Noah.

"Taking the lead again," the announcer said, "is Susie Boston." He paused. "And there seems to be some confusion over skier thirty-one, Noah French. We believe he may have missed a turn and skied off the trail. We'll bring you more information as soon as it's available."

"Oh, my." Mrs. French's hand shook as she pointed toward the screen. "That's the same turn he missed last year when he had that hor-hor-horrible accident."

"We've got to get up there!" Beka said as she flew to the door, still clutching Noah's book. While the Frenches pulled on shoes and jackets, Beka set the book on a hall table. Sparking white, it reappeared with no one noticing.

Out the door they flew, and into the car. Beka hustled inside before the door slammed. Seconds later, the car bounced and lurched along the snow-packed drive.

Hunching in the back seat, Beka concentrated on the sound of tires crunching crusty snow.

It took her mind off what they might find when they got to Walrus Mountain.

And, it distracted her from listening to Mrs. French's foreboding comments about "history repeating itself."

20
Going for the Gold

Robbie opened his eyes and stared at sunbeams filtering through the pine boughs under which he landed. Thatch stood over him, nudging his face with a wet nose, as if trying to make him move.

"Leave me alone," Robbie groaned. Every time he closed his eyes, he relived those last terrifying moments: Flying through the air, hitting snow-covered branches; sliding to a mushy landing.

He was afraid to get up. Afraid of what he might find — Noah, with two broken legs.

"Robbie? Thatch? Are you here?" came Noah's voice.

Robbie lifted his head.

Noah was not laid out flat with broken skis —

and legs. He was digging in the snow under one of the trees.

"Woof!" Thatch loved digging. In seconds he was helping. And the snow was disappearing.

"You *are* here," Noah exclaimed, watching the snow disappear, then reappear in a pile behind them. "Good boy. Keep digging."

Noah leaned back to survey the area. "Rob, I don't know where you landed, but you're probably wondering what happened."

"It crossed my mind," Robbie muttered, getting up and brushing off the snow.

"I did this on purpose."

"You *what?*" Robbie wished Noah could hear him so he could give the boy a piece of his mind.

"I don't expect you to understand." Noah addressed the grove of evergreens, assuming the ghost was there. "But the hardest part of this whole day was stepping into those skis and going up that lift. Pulling on the number and taking my place at the start. And hearing Zip Boston call me Grindelwald."

He shrugged and went back to helping Thatch dig. "Once I survived *those* things, I was fine. I was my old self again. Taking the lead didn't surprise me. I even *lost* the lead, then won it back. From *her.*"

He grinned, remembering. "I did it, Rob. I did what I've been afraid to do for a whole year."

"Then why are we sitting here in the snow instead of sailing across the finish line past a cheering crowd?"

"So, you're probably wondering why I didn't finish the race. Well, the whole time I was skiing, all I could think about was the gold medallion."

"Thank you. I had something to do with that." Robbie was pleased that his mental suggestions had been so successful.

"Then, when I headed down the stretch where my accident happened, all I wanted to do was come back here and find that medal."

"Nooooo!" Robbie sputtered. "I wasn't talking about *that* medallion, I was talking about *your* medallion. The one *you're* supposed to win."

"I know I can win my *own* gold. If not this year, then next. Right now it's more important that I find my dad's medal."

"Ah, that explains the digging."

They dug for a good half hour before they found it.

Summer's thaw had deposited the medal at the base of a tree. Winter's many snows had buried it at least four feet.

The blue ribbon was ruined — faded and shredded. But the gold shone bright, making the walrus's tusks gleam in the sunshine. Engraved under the walrus was:

First Place Winner
Avery Morrell French
Walrus Mountain Junior Ski Race
1972

"Wow," Robbie said. "It's nifty."

Noah held it in his hands a long time before he folded the ribbon and slipped it into his pocket. "Better get out of here before the ski patrol comes looking for me."

Robbie thought the boy wiped a tear as he said it.

Noah stepped into his skis and paused for Robbie to climb on board.

"Let's go, Thatch!" Noah called.

Thatch bounded over to him.

"Hey," Robbie teased. "He's *my* dog, not yours. *I'll* tell him when to come."

But Thatch was already off down the hill, leading the way home.

21
The Final Message

The twins lounged around Noah's room, watching him pack.

He'd carried a plate of pizza upstairs for lunch, but doggy-sized bites kept disappearing.

Robbie wondered how long it would take Noah to notice the vanishing pizza.

Around the boy's neck hung the gold walrus medallion. He and his father had gone into Juniper last night and shopped for a new blue ribbon to replace the ruined one.

There'd been a lot of hugging and crying at the foot of the mountain after he and Noah coasted across the finish line.

When Noah's father heard the reason for the detour, he seemed prouder of his son than he would have been if Noah had won the race.

First place went to Zip Boston. No surprise to anyone. Her brother Chip had come in ninth, after losing half a tooth to a boulder he claimed jumped out in front of him on the home stretch.

"*Next* year," Noah had told everyone. "Just wait till next year."

"Hurry, Son," came Mr. French's voice from downstairs. "We need to get on the road."

"Coming, Dad," Noah called back. "I have to pack my computer."

But instead, he turned it on. "I suspect you ghost guys are here," Noah began. "If you are, I want to thank you, and Thatch, too. I never would've done what I did yesterday if you guys hadn't bugged me so much." He laughed to show it was okay. "Is there anything I can do for *you* before I leave?"

"Mmmmm," Beka said. She let go of the balloon Robbie had brought her from the carnival. It sparked pink as it became visible and bobbed against the ceiling.

"I know." Robbie moved to the computer. LEEV PIZZA.

"Really?"

The message reminded Noah of his own lunch. He reached for the plate. All the pizza was gone except a couple of bites. "Bad dog!" he teased, then tossed the rest onto the floor and watched it disappear.

"That's it?" Noah asked. "Pizza is all you want?"
SODA 2
"You got it."

"Noah! We're leaving!"

Quickly he unplugged the computer and packed it away. Grabbing his suitcase, he stopped at the door. "Thanks again, ghosts. Ski you next year. I mean — " he stopped to laugh at his mistake, "*see* you next year."

Robbie thought there was a lot of truth in his slip of the tongue.

Minutes later the Frenches finished packing the car. Before they pulled out, Noah made up an excuse to run back into the house. His real reason, of course, was to smuggle back the leftover pizza and soda his mom had wrapped for the trip home. Then the family was gone.

"Come on," Beka said. "It's been fifty years since we last ate lunch."

Thatch was the first one down the stairs.

"Not *you*," Robbie hollered, racing the dog to the kitchen. "You already had a bite of pizza."

But Thatch didn't care. The twins *still* had to fight him for their share.

Rules to be Ghosts by . . .

1. Ghosts can touch objects, but not people or animals. Our hands go right through them.
2. Ghosts can cause "a disturbance" around people to get their attention. Here are three ways: walk through them; yell and scream a lot; chant a message over and over.
3. Rules of the world don't apply to ghosts.
4. Thatch's ghost-dog powers are stronger than ours. He can do things we can't. Sometimes he even teaches us things we didn't know we could do.
5. Ghosts can't move through closed doors, walls, or windows (but we can *smoosh* through if there is one tiny hole).
6. Ghosts don't need to eat, but they can if they want to.
7. Ghosts can listen in on other people's conversations.
8. Ghosts can move objects by concentrating on them until they move into the other dimension and become invisible. When we let go of the object, it becomes visible again.
9. Ghosts don't need to sleep, but can rest by "floating." If our energy is drained (by too much haunting or *smooshing*) we must re-

turn to Kickingbird Lake to renew our strength.

10.   Ghosts can move from one place to another by thinking hard about where we want to be, and wishing it. Thatch must be there for it to work.

Don't Miss!
The Missing Moose Mystery —
GHOST TWINS #4

Thatch gave a growl-bark, sounding like he meant business. Like he was telling *whatever* not to follow, or IT would have an angry ghost dog to deal with.

Beka bolted. All she could think about was getting out of there. Getting to safety.

Thatch galloped behind, racing so close he almost tripped her.

Rounding the last corner, Beka flew toward the gate.

It was closed.

She gasped. The gate had been open when she entered the cemetery.

How was she supposed to get out? The gate was ten feet high.

She slowed, but Thatch kept moving. In one smooth leap, he sailed over the fence.

"Wow!" Beka watched in awe.

Then it hit her. Thatch was *outside* — but *she* was still *inside*. Trapped.

On the other side of the fence Thatch paced, acting confused.

Grasping the iron bars, horror sent dizziness flooding through until she felt faint. Was IT pounding the drive after her?

Terrified, Beka screamed, "Puppy, don't leave me here!"

About the Author

Ms. Regan is from Colorado Springs and graduated from the University of Colorado in Boulder. Presently, she lives in Edmond, Oklahoma, sharing an office with her cat, Poco, seventy-two walruses, and a growing collection of ghosts.